To
AIDEN,

From

Aidan Geovahni Garaq

You may have heard the stories?
I tell you they are true!
A superhero lives nearby.
But where? I wish I knew!

WHO
IS

OUR
HERO?

He's got an "A" upon his suit,
His cape is long and flowing.

Who is the boy behind the mask?
There's just no way of knowing!

They say he's very clever.
He's brave and fast and strong.
Do you know who he is yet?
His name's FIVE letters long!

SUPER DUPER CLUES

- He wears a mask
- He can fly—sort of!
- He's about this tall:
- His name is A _ _ _ _

Oh no! A cat's stuck up a tree!
But who will get it out?
Our hero stops and says,
"I'll use my. . .

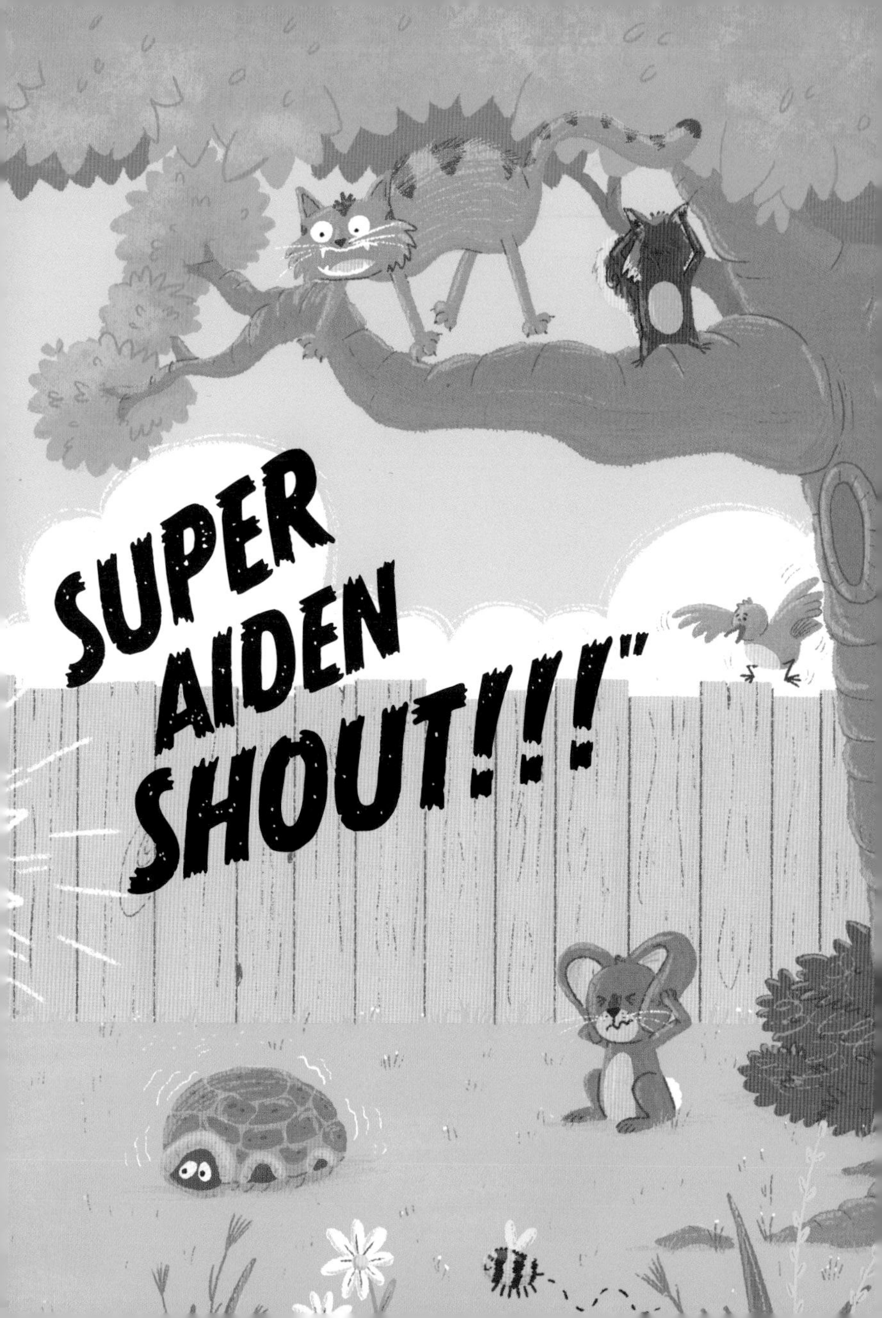
SUPER
AIDEN
SHOUT!!!"

This little girl is crying.
Her trike has got a flat.

I guess it must be hungry work
When one is fighting crime.
He runs and jumps and dives around.
He's moving all the time!

HOT DOGS

Super Aiden is so strong,
He simply can't be beaten.
It must be all the salad, sprouts,
And broccoli he's eaten!

There's trouble on the playground!
Kids start to scream and shout.

Super Aiden, kind and true,
Knows how to work this out!

He's the world's best superhero.
And he's got a super cuddle!

The next time you're in trouble,
Or ever in harm's way, shout. . .

This superhero stuff's hard work,
And now he's very sleepy,
But Super Aiden feels afraid–
His bedroom looks so creepy!

Yet heroes do not run or hide
When they are feeling scared!
Instead they face their fears head on.
That's why he's come prepared!

He's always super-wonderful.
He's super-terrific, too.
Just who is Super Aiden?
WAIT! I think it must be...

Loves video games
Awesome at capture the flag
Awesome at writing
Awesome at making Friends
Runs Fast
Smart Person

Written by Eric James
Illustrated by Steve Brown
Designed by Ryan Dunn

Copyright © Hometown World Ltd 2018

Put Me In The Story is a
registered trademark of Sourcebooks, Inc.
All rights reserved.

Published by Put Me In The Story,
a publication of Sourcebooks, Inc.
P.O. Box 4410, Naperville, Illinois 60567-4410
(630) 961-3900
www.putmeinthestory.com

Date of Production: October 2018
Run Number: HTW_PO201833
Printed and bound in Italy (LG)
10 9 8 7 6 5 4 3 2 1

put *me*
in the **story**®

Bestselling books starring your child!
www.putmeinthestory.com